JOE JOE

JOE JOE

Mary Serfozo   illustrated by Nina S. Montezinos

MARGARET K. McELDERRY BOOKS
New York

Maxwell Macmillan Canada
Toronto

Maxwell Macmillan International
New York Oxford Singapore Sydney

OTHER BOOKS BY MARY SERFOZO

WHO SAID RED? *illustrated by Keiko Narahashi*
WHO WANTS ONE? *illustrated by Keiko Narahashi*
RAIN TALK *illustrated by Keiko Narahashi*
DIRTY KURT *illustrated by Nancy Poydar*
BENJAMIN BIGFOOT *illustrated by Jos. A. Smith*

ALSO ILLUSTRATED BY NINA S. MONTEZINOS

LOOK! SNOW! *by Kathryn O. Galbraith*

(MARGARET K. McELDERRY BOOKS)

Margaret K. McElderry Books   Maxwell Macmillan Canada, Inc.
Macmillan Publishing Company   1200 Eglinton Avenue East
866 Third Avenue   Suite 200
New York, NY 10022   Don Mills, Ontario M3C 3N1

Macmillan Publishing Company is part of the Maxwell Communication Group of Companies.
First edition
Printed in Singapore   10 9 8 7 6 5 4 3 2 1
The text of this book is set in ITC Novarese Medium. The illustrations are rendered in pastel, colored pencil, and oil stick.

Library of Congress Cataloging-in-Publication Data
Serfozo, Mary.
   Joe Joe / Mary Serfozo : illustrated by Nina S. Montezinos. — 1st ed.   p.   cm.
   Summary: During an active outing, Joe Joe produces such sounds as "Bang bang," "Clap clap," and "Splash splash."
   ISBN 0-689-50578-7
   [1. Sound—Fiction.]   I. Montezinos, Nina, ill.   II. Title.
PZ7.S482Jo   1993   [E]—dc20   92-30133

For Jacqi, because old friends are best
—M.S.

To Joe Joe Joe Joe Joe…a million times to Joe
—N.S.M.

bang

bong

clang

clap

hop

squish

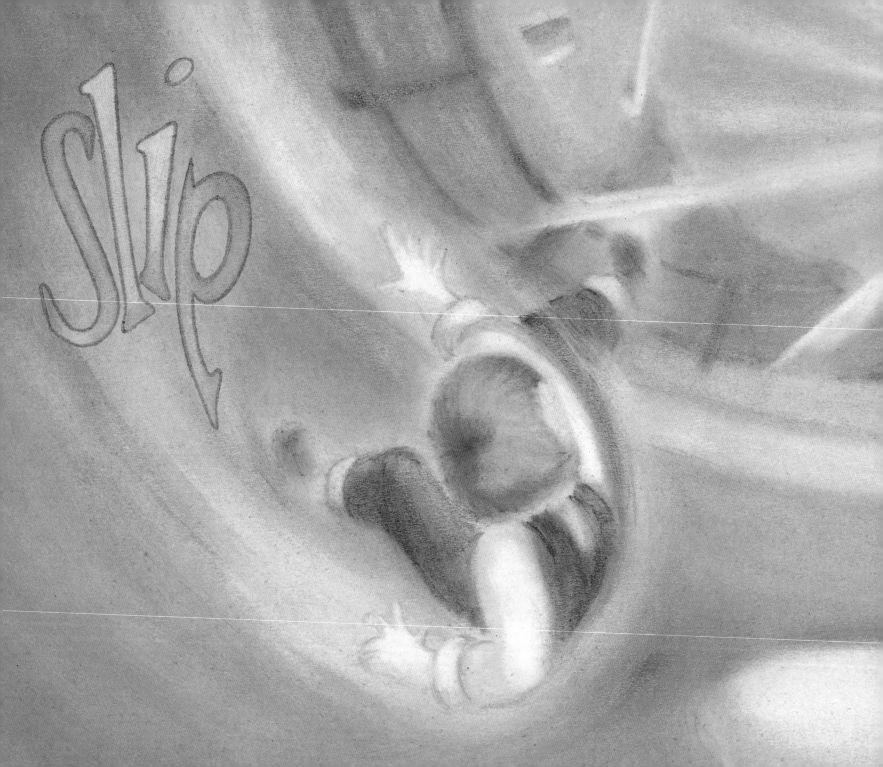

slip

drip

drip

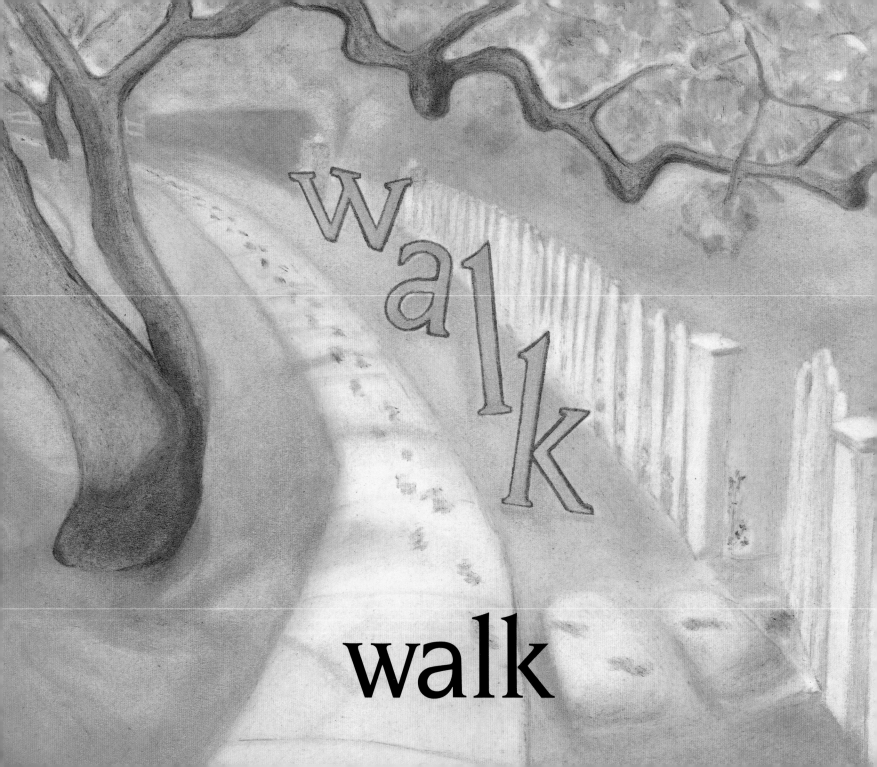

walk

back

go

slow

slow

oh!

oh!